707
(Sci-fiction)

R.Sathia Narayanan (2016)

Published by

Invincible Publishers
www.i-publish.in

Title   :   7 O' 7 (Sci-fiction)

Copyright   :   R.Sathia Narayanan

Published by   :   Invincible Publishers
                            Opp Kasturba Gandhi Ashram
                            Radaur, Haryana- 135133

Typeset by   :   K. Balasundaram

Cover Design   :   Ravi Verma

Edition   :   First

ISBN no   :   978-81-932382-6-4

About the Author

R.Sathia Narayanan is a Maths Graduate. Right from the College days he was a Revolutionary both in thought and Action. He worked in Indian Telephones Department for few years and left the job for becoming a Full Time Revolutionary.

In 1980's he has created and directed hundreds of Street-plays and conducted it successfully on Stage and Streets throughout Tamil Nadu. But this did not last long. He left his ideology because of Psychological, family and social reasons.

Then, he gradually transformed into a Humanist with Spirituality. But his rational and scientific thinking never ceased. He worked as a Sub-Editor of "Punnagai Ulagam" a student's monthly from 2009 to 2011. He made contributions on world famous scientists, Mendel, Hubble, and Aryabhatta and so on. One of his articles in the magazine titled " The Turning Point" illustrated the Invention of Zero by Indians was the Gate way to Modern Science and Technology.

In the same year he presented a paper for International Conference on Science and Religion titled "Philosophy : The Science of all Sciences". It is thought provoking.

After that, though he lived in uttermost adverse financial conditions, his love for Humanism and Scientific thinking never ceased. His passion for writing also never ceased. With great difficulties he brought 2 books in Tamil. Till today his love for Humanism and rational scientific thinking and Love for Scientist and Science is going strong.

This fiction is a manifestation of his love and imagination towards Science and Humanism!

Preface

I dedicate this fiction to my late parents Gomathy and Ramamurthy. My sincere thanks to the Publishers, Artists, and the Press people.

I thank Ramani, Malathy, Sabarish and Vidhya and my Sisters for their help and contributions.

Thanks to all.
Dear readers….
Kids…
Boys and Girls…
Students and Youth…
And all….

WISH U A HAPPY READING!

SATHYAN
13TH MARCH, 2016

Inside...

7 o' 7 BEGINNING

7

6

5

4

3

2

1

0 !

The countdown of a Space Ship begins this way.

Yes. Zero !

0.

It is the starting point. If a student is asked to narrate the numerals, he begins it with one (1) ! It is wrong. It is against basic mathematics.

Why?

Actually take one (1). It is the smallest of all positive integers. That is the numerals start with one (1). Is it so?

Certainly not. When you divide'0' by one (1) the answer is '0'. That's okay. But when we divide one (1) by '0' the answer is INFINITY.

WHAT DOES IT MEAN ? If you divide the smallest number by the smallest number you get infinity. That is large, uncountable and undeterminable!

From this we get, zero is not equal to NOTHING.

Zero=0=SOMETHING

You may even say it is mystic or Magical!! Leave it there.

The birth of Universe (The Big Bang Theory) is certainly not from NOTHING. Nothing can come out from Nothing. Something has to come from something. So for anything there is a starting point like Zero. So, zero is not equal to Nothing but it is actually SOMETHING!!!

YES. Without zero, there is no Maths. No higher Maths. This has been proved already. So zero is the starting point of numerals.

Yes...it is 0...1...2...3...4...5...6...7

So anything begins with '0' that is 'Something'. So let us begin the Chapter '0' of this Sci-fiction. Here let us take a mathematical rule. Two parallel lines meet at infinity. Can you imagine this?

See...the railway lines are parallel . But will they meet at some point? We can easily say that the railway lines will not meet at any point. But this is though looks like truth actually it is not. Higher

Maths has proved that the 2 parallel lines meet at infinity. This has been verified and applied in Higher Maths. It may look silly…

But it is a FACT!

Yes. 2 parallel lines meet at infinity. Now let us imagine 2 planets which are parallel to each other travelling in space. What can we infer from this? The 2 planets will meet at some point at infinity. This is not imaginary but the TRUTH.

Okay. This is not a Maths text book. This is not a Research document.

This is the 'ZERO' of the novel 7 O' 7!!!

What is 7 O' 7? Let us begin the countdown of the Sci-fiction…

Yes…the countdown begins….

7

6

5

4

3

2

1

2216 A.D!!!

01. 2116 A.D!

2000 + 100 + 10 + 6=2116 A.D!

It is 22nd century. Humans have traversed a long time and long period. Let us first have a bird's eye view of the 22nd century. It is totally NEW. It is positive. Humans have enough time to study and research Nature. To mention specifically humans are trying to explore Space and Time!

Before we go in to the fiction or story, let us have a good picture of our planet. There are no more Global Villages…We have only global Cities and Towns.

Our Globe…

Our Planet…

Our Mother Earth…

Is called the Blue Planet!

Yes.

We live in Blue Planet.

In 2116 A.D…

Let us take 07 departments and let us peep in to the actual conditions of the Society. This is not 21st century. This is 22nd!

A beautiful place to live!

A paradise in Reality!! All well in Blue planet!!!

Let us briefly go in to the details of 2116 A.D…

The 7 departments in the Society are :

    01.   **People**
    02.   **State**
    03.   **Universal Economy**
    04.   **Technology and Communication**
    05.   **Environment and Space Research**
    06.   **Education**
    07.   **Medical Facility.**
    08.   **Art and Entertainment**

We will see each briefly…

00. PEOPLE

All people of the Blue Planet are happy. No problems what so ever. They love peace and humanity. They are duty conscious. They work hard for 8s and relax themselves for 8 hours. And most of the People sleep from 7 to 8 hours.

Though the Blue Planet has very defined Nations the boundaries of nations are withering away. It is not a planned one. But people they themselves break the barriers of nations and are voluntarily forming Federation of Nations.

    No war.
    No terrorism.
    No robbery.
    No rape.
    No crimes.
    Yes. It is the Paradise! It is the heaven!!

02. STATE

Let us be Particular.

We are in NAVA BHARATH!

It is nothing but India in the last century. But a total silent revolution has taken place in the mid and end of 21st century. Ya...It is great! There are no villages!!!

All are Towns!!! Agricultural Towns, Cities and Metro Cities... that's all. There are 7 major Metro cities.....

01. O1. DEL   (derived from 21sr century Delhi)
02. KOL   (derived from Kolkata)
03. MUMB (derived from Mumbai)
04. CHEN (derived from Chennai)
05. HYD   (derived from Hyderabad)
06. BANG (derived from Bangalore)
07. OOTY (derived from OOTY)

CHEN is the capital of Nava Bharath. And it is globally connected to the core. It is one of the largest Metro cities in the Nava Bharath. It is the capital of Paradise! It is nothing but Heaven!!

The highest body of the State is House of Executives. They meet at Chen and Ooty periodically. There is no Parliament. There are no poetical parties. Yes....It is great! No M.P.s and M.L.A.s and we have only M.Ex.s who are none other than paid workers. They must be educated and pass an Administrative exam. This is mandatory. Moreover, at least for 4 years they must have worked for People and Society in anyway and in any department voluntarily. There will be elections and people will elect the M.Ex.s. And they form the House of Executives. People not only elect but also they have the right to Re-call any M.Ex.s. if his work is not up to the satisfaction. All the power to People only.

True Democracy…

True Socialistic…

Corruption closed…

A New chapter has begun!

02. How People lived?

Let us see what the Economy of Nava Bharath and the Globe. The Economic specialists call 22nd century Economy of all nations as UNIVERSAL ECONOMY.

Oh!

What is Universal Economy?

First of all there is NO MONEY! No coins!!

It is the first ever Great Revolution of Blue Planet and it was lead by Nava Bharath a few decades ago. What has really happened?

A great Green Revolution!(Agriculture) !

A great White Revolution (Diary) !!

Most importantly there is No Employment Exchanges. No unemployment problem at all. All are given work. All are 'paid'. And what is the payment ?

Certainly not money!

The state gives WC…i.e….Work Card. It has 5 divisions only. That is from *1 to *5.

There are no Banks. We have only Commodity Storage Banks, shortly they are called CSBs. They keep account of all produced products and look in to the aspects of distribution to people through WCs.

If you give your monthly provision purchase list to the Bank and give your WC..say *2... they will order the products to be delivered to your house and some points in your WC would be reduced. You can save much 'Points' every month and you can use it to buy costly electronic gadgets.

In Society...

No beggars...

No prostitutes...

No criminals...

No illiteracy...

No unemployment...

No corruption...

No evils...

That is enough for you to understand what actually 2116 is all about.

03. Environment and Space Research

The Global Warming is taken in to account. All preventive measures are taken. The Ozone layer is protected. The El Nino effect is minimized. The Global Revolution in Earth or Blue Planet was lead by Nava Bharath. Yes...Nava Bharath is a Super, Super Power, SSP! There is now water, air, soil or noise pollution anywhere. The noise pollution...i.e....greater than the specified decibels is allowed on National Holidays. But for expect Mass Fire Works in cities and towns ...there is no absolute pollution.

SPACR RESEARCH

O! My goodness!! What a development...NASA and ESA have fallen terrifically to ISRO. Though the name India was changed to

Nava Bharath, the name of Indian Space Research Organization… ISRO is not changed. It is still ISRO only. ISRO is the pioneer and leader in Space Research. It has sent lots of Satellites to Space. It has sent successfully humans to Moon, Mars and Space. ISRO has had a Great Leap Forward! ISRO is the king of Space Research in the Blue Planet. ISRO has 70 observation centers all around the world/ Globe. It has many Major Space Launching Stations in 7 Major Nava Bharath Metro cities. The launching stations are at the outskirts of Metro Cities.

People salute ISRO!

03. What else?

Education!

Education is compulsory. But it is FREE to all. No reservations. Open to all at all levels. The education pattern is not the old Memorizing Pattern. Memorizing is only a little part of Education. It is totally Scientific and Logical. Right from the age of 3 kids starts Schooling. They are taught with playing materials and interesting practical. Kids voluntarily get involved in the Education System and they LOVE it to the core. The education from Elementary, High school and at Colleges and Universities is absolutely FREE! The pattern is as follows :

$$3 + 8 + 4 + 3 + 2....$$

That is lower classes from 3 years. Elementary up to 8 years. Pre-University 4 years. Post-graduation 3 years and for Research 2 years.

Fantastic! Is not it?

In Nava Bharath…

There are 70 Universities which are graded accordingly. Graduation courses are plenty. There are about 700 courses at Pre-University levels. From Maths to Life Sciences and Information Technology (IT) to Space Research and so on and so forth. The most sought course under Medicine is Genetic Engineering. All the courses are technically associated. Students do not learn….they understands the Theory and practical at all levels. From basic sciences to Medicine and

Engineering students are allowed to take Specialization according to their interests.

THERE IS NO COMPETITION WHAT SO EVER!

Right from the beginning students,

> READ
>
> UNDERSTAND
>
> DO PRACTICALS
>
> CHANCE GIVEN TO NEW AND INNOVATIVE IDEAS

The beauty of Education is that it transforms all the students to become as Scientists! In all 700 fields and departments. 100% literacy! To tell about the linguistics much importance is given to English, Tamil and Sanskrit. A few decades ago there was a Renaissance in Sanskrit. Throughout the Globe, ever one accepts the fact that Samskrit is a Logical and Scientifical language. And study of it highly increases the I.Q. of the students.

'Baghu Uthamam!'....yes....very GOOD!!

05. Medical Facility.

All the Metro cities and towns have Multi Specialty Hospitals. It is owned by people that is State-less state. More importantly all the Medical Facilities to common man are absolutely FREE!! Even all the Medicines are FREE!!!

Starting from normal cold to Cancer, Heart Attack, and Stroke... everything is treated with CARE and HOSPITABILITY. Absolutely Free. Open heart-surgery, open Brain Surgery and Organ transplantation are smartly done. As expected there was a Medical Revolution in the last decade of the last century.(21st) But a new thing is advancing in the 22nd century. That is Gene Transplantation! It is the 22nd century invention! it cures diseases and makes humans live long. This

Gene Transplantation can be done to a patient only once…and before he/she is 50.

What's the use?

THEY WILL LIVE FOR 200 YEARS!!! GURANTEED!!!

It is a costly operation. People with *3 ,*4,and *5 can do it immediately. But people with *1 and *2 have to register and wait. It may take few years…! It is better to register as early as possible. Done!

The main Medical system has 2 systems. Namely, Allopathic and Ayurveda. And there is Homeopathy too…for prolonged diseases. Ayurveda is clinically tested and observed and medicines are prepared as per very old Ayurveda text books by Indian Saints, who were Ayurveda doctors. Both Allopath and Ayurveda move parallel to each other though both are differently based. People can select their own medical system. They are given freedom. They are explained about various systems, their history, achievements etc.

Mental health plays an important part. Both PHYSICAL and MENTAL health are given due importance and RECOVERY in a quick span of time is achieved.

Yes…

Health is Wealth!

Take care of yourself!!

Get cured!!! Be Strong. Okay?

04. Relax!

$8 h$ours work.

8 hours relax.

8 hours sleep…

Yes…

8 hours is for relaxing! What do they do in these 8 hours? They read, play, and involve themselves in some hobbies. Mental relaxation is given uttermost importance. Right from age 1 to till the death people are engaged in some kind of ACTIVITY. Even cooking is considered to be a hobby.

Next comes 2 departments.

06. Technology and Communication

The 21st century witnessed a global Revolution in Technology. There are only, mainly 2 things. Information Technology (IT) through INTERNET bloomed like anything. The software and the Hardware of the computers were revolutionized at regular intervals. People used mostly SMART phones and a lot of 3-D movies got released worldwide in the latter part of the 21st century. Though Tech and Communication is the main part of Economy…next to agriculture…i.e….Universal Economy, its use is largely felt in People's relaxing hours. Yes…They meet Tech and communication at work Places. But the main Revolution was outside the work places. Now, no Mobiles…We have AV Boxes. It is 3cm x 3cm x 3cm pocket AUDIO-VIDEO Box. You can talk to anyone in the world with this one. It is the Revolutionized version of SMART phones of the 21st Century. The Video conferencing too can be held through the AV Boxes. You have bigger AV Boxes too! You can interact with anyone face to face. It can also take very high resolution photos with very high pixels. You can MSG, CALL and take snaps from the AV Box. Also you have INTERNET and OUTERNET in these AV Boxes. You can take a Film for 7 minutes in this Box. There is Editing software too. You can edit, mix, and re-record. Yes…Crores of such 7 minutes Films have been taken throughout the world.

The main tool of the 22nd century is PC Box. PC means not personal Computer. But it is actually POCKET COMPUTER. Its dimensions are 7cm x 5cm x 1cm. It is more than a computer. It has OUTERNET! Outer net means viewing Space. Yes…you can view planets, sun, moon and other satellites…completely owing to space. Everything connected to SPACE. And this is the OUTERNET.

Oh! What next?

7-D Theatres!!! !!! ! Have you ever heard of it? It is the most common Cinema Theatres with 7D facility. What is 7D? It has 7 dimensions…

      01.   Length
      02.   Breadth
      03.   Depth
      04.   Odor
      05.   Real Audio
      06.   Movement/Motion
      07.   Special effects

3D was the norm of the 21st century. But in 22nd century the norm is 7D. So theatres are differently built. It is like a semi-circle. You have to lie at 450 in the seat. That is the screen is inclined to 450 to the floor. Actually you are in semi-lying position. Almost like in a hospital bed. But where is the screen? It is ABOVE you. It is not rectangular…but a CURVED screen top of you. You have to watch the movie lying down only. 3D everyone knows pretty well. The 4D is odor. That is if the Hero enters the fish market you can feel…or smell the fish. If the heroine enters a flower shop you can smell the Jasmine.

Next is Real Audio. (RA)

If it rains in the sky (Screen)…you will hear the sound of rain as if you are caught up in the rain…Terrible…isn't it?

If you are watching a Bullet train travelling at 600km/hour…you will hear the noise nearby you in the theatre. Incredible!

And the 6th D is motion.

It cannot be imagined. Instead you will have to FEEL it. If the hero is going in a bus, you will feel that you are going in a bus. The seat which was originally 450 will stand erect at 900. You will be sitting in this scene and FEEL travelling in a bus exactly. The same with a boat or ship. Imagine Space Travel scene…

Oh! Oh!! Oh!!! The 6th D is terrific!!!

What is the 7th D?

Special effects. Suppose an Earth-quake occurs in the film the seat will vibrate to the exact feeling of earthquake. What an experience! Suppose a Tsunami occurs in the film, a huge chill wave will be split on your body…Oh! That's great!!

7-D is the norm of the 22nd century.

07. Art and Entertainment

The mass entertainment is &-D movies. Movies are totally revolutionized in content and form. More and more regarding Science, Religion and Space are taken artistically and released. People engage in some form of ART, say Rangoli, drawing, painting, painting 3=D pictures etc. Music is all time Relaxing hobby. Dancing and Exercises have become common to all common man. Yoga, Kung-fu, Karate and Kalari has become global hobbies. Yoga stands first. In dancing Bharatha Natyam has itself revolutionized in contemporary themes. No more repetitions of peacock, Krishna dance etc. Journalism is all time favorite of Intellectuals. Writing to magazines starts from the age of 5. Many love to write!

Of course millions love to read!!

Yes…that's the way to RELAX those 8 hours!!!

05. Most important

We have worked 8 hours…

We have relaxes 8 hours…

Now…it is time to sleep. Good night!! Sweet dreams!!! Sleep well. Relax your body and mind. Awake. Be fresh. Start a new day. Have a nice day. Always adhere to your Biological Clock. Never try to change it permanently. Do work…Have fun…But never forget or skip Sleeping. Sleep is the pre-condition to freshness and alertness.

Sleep…sleep…sleep!!!

06. Family Bio-data

FATHER

01.	Name	:	SRI
02.	Gender	:	Male
03.	Age	:	44
04.	Address	:	No7, Shastha Apts, K7 road, CHEN-087
05.	Qualification	:	Ph.d
06.	Profession	:	Software Engineer at ISRO
07.	Specialization	:	Vehicle Launching & Satellites
08.	Personality	:	Extrovert, Humble & Sincere
09.	Blood group	:	O +ve
10.	Gene Main		DNA 108
11.	AV Box No	:	0723467
12.	Card status	:	WC *5 (Work Card Star 5)
13.	Hobbies	:	Cooking, writing, reading & Cricket
14.	Interests	:	Space Research
15.	Any other info	:	A great orator A great writer

MOTHER

01.	Name	:	BEN
02.	Gender	:	Female
03.	Age	:	39

04.	Address	:	No.7, Shastha Apts, K7 Road, CHEN-087
05.	Qualification	:	Ph.d
06.	Profession	:	Hardware Engineer ISRO
07.	Specialization	:	Satellite Launching & Monitoring Space
08.	Personality	:	Humble, Creative, Fast and Efficient
09.	Blood group	:	A +ve
10.	Gene Main		DNA 786
11.	AV Box No	:	0714556
12.	Card Status	:	WC *5 (Work Card Star 5)
13.	Hobbies	:	Swimming, painting & Research on Sun
14.	Interests	:	Sun, space & flying machines
15.	Any other info	:	A great Scholar. Good in Electronics. Loves too much the Kids.

DAUGHTER

01.	Name	:	VIVI
02.	Gender	:	Female
03.	Age	:	13
04.	Address	:	Refer Sri's Address
05.	Qualification	:	8th Forum
06.	Profession	:	Student
07.	Specialization	:	Electronics & Communications
08.	Personality	:	Hyper Active and Prodigy
09.	Blood Group	:	A1 +ve
10.	Gene main	:	DNA 077
11.	AV box No	:	078423
12.	Card Status	:	MINOR WC *5
13.	Hobbies	:	Outernet, Internet, Photography Reading GENETICS
14.	Interests	:	Maths, Astronomy, Chemistry,

			Genetic Engineering
15.	Any other info	:	A great Chemist. A Maths Genius A child Prodigy. Awarded Junior Space Scientist by ISRO.

SON

01.	Name	:	SABU
02.	Gender	:	Male
03.	Age	:	09
04.	Address	:	Refer BEN's address
05.	Qualification	:	4th Forum
06.	Profession	:	Student
07.	Specialization	:	Space Science
08.	Personality	:	Sharp, Extrovert and Brilliant
09.	Blood Group	:	AB
10.	Gene main		DNA 314
11.	AV Box NO	:	0758341
12.	Card Status	:	Minor WC *5
13.	Hobbies	:	Cooking, Doing experiments, Outernet, Sun & Space, and
14.			Working on NUMBERS
15.	Interests	:	Space, Genetics, Maths, Cycling
16.			Foot Ball and Table Tennis
17.	Any other info	:	A champion in Table Tennis Awarded Junior Space Scientist By ISRO. A Prodigy.

———•◆•———

07. Wedding Anniversary

February 29th, 2116.

The 4th wedding anniversary of Sri and Ben.

Just a minute…

Sri and Ben have a 13 year old girl (VIVI) and a 9 year old Son (SABU) ! How come this possible? Parents are celebrating just the 4th anniversary…but they have 13 year and9 year old kids! How come? Is it a contradiction…or wrong somewhere?

NO.

NO.

NO.

There is no contradiction. Sri and Ben got married on February 29th, 2100!

2100 is a Leap year.

2116 is also a Leap Year. They got married on Feb 29th. So…they celebrated 1st anniversary only after 4 years i.e. on 2104! The 2nd 2108. The 3rd 2112. Hence…

4th wedding anniversary in 2116!

Yes. Feb 29th. It comes only once in 4 years…isn't it? Yes…in 16 years they have celebrated their Anniversary only 4 times!

So…today Feb 29th is…Sri & Ben's 4th wedding anniversary!! (2116).

The flat 007 is in festive mood. The ceremony is conducted in the terrace of the building. All the friends of Sri, Ben, Vivi and Sabu have assembled. The flat mates have also come. A thick brown Chocolate Cake is on the table. Sri & Ben jointly cut the cake. Vivi distributes the cake to all. Sabu distributes the ALLVITA cool drink bottles to all. It is a All Vitamins cool energy drink which is a product of 22nd century. It comes in 7 flavors. It is AllVitta! Vivi takes apple flavored and Sabu takes the Pine-apple flavored. Just a simple get-to-gather. All the participants communicate with each other and talk about the current affairs of Nava Bharath.

Just 2 hours. It's all over. Sri & Ben take leave and tell the kids that they will be back in an hour. Sabu starts cooking. Vivi browses the OUTERNET. After an hour Vivi and Sabu are drinking the Cool ice Tea with lemon. It is really refreshing. Sri and Ben return. They enter the flat. Sri gives a small presentation to Vivi and Ben gives a small parcel as gift to Sabu. The kids are extremely happy. Both of them shout…

"O! Wav! What is it?"

08. All-in-All Watch

Flat 007.

Vivi and Sabu are in jubilant mood. They tear the wrapper of the gift box. Ben tells in a soft voice…

"See…Sabu and Vivi…you have manuals inside. Read it carefully and make use of this properly. You know what it is ?"

In the mean time Vivi and Sabu take 2 wrist watches. Sabu's watch is red. Vivi's is yellow one. On seeing the watch Sabu shouts…

"Hey…it is an ALL-in-ALL Watch…Oh! Fantastic!!"

Vivi in excited mood shouts…

"O! Dad and Mum…It is a nice gift. Aha! I love All-in-All Watch! Thanks a lot to both of you…O! O! My goodness…I have an ALL-in-ALL Watch…"

Sri and Ben leave the hall. Vivi and Sabu start exploring the watch. Sabu says…

"Vivi from 00 to 13…it has 14 buttons…O! So small…Come on let us put it on our wrists…"

Sabu and Vivi tie the watch in their wrists. They are very happy and took the manuals and kept them on their studying table. So what now? Just playing with the watch. Sabu presses the button no. 3. The watch shows:

Blood fasting Sugar = 81mgs/l

Blood PP	=	147mgs/l
RESULT	=	Normal

Sabu with excitement shouts….

"My blood sugar is normal…" and continues "What a Beauty!"

Now Vivi presses the button 07. And the screen in the watch with a beep sound types as :

B.P.	=	125/81
Result	=	Normal

Vivi shouts…

"My B. P. is normal…what a beauty!"

Sabu presses the key 05. The watch shows the map as below :

****

Result	:	Total Normal.

Sabu shouts :

"Vivi…my ECG is Normal"

"Fantastic…Vivi you are a hyperactive…so it is better you browse your EEG…Come on…What is the button for EEG? See… in the manual…"

Vivi replies :

"It is 07…"

Sabu… "Come on press 07…". Vivi presses 07 and a map is displayed :

****

Result	:	Hyperactive
Suggestion	:	Take plenty of Water.
		Avoid extreme sugar.

Sabu in excitement jumps high and high. Actually he is experimenting something. Vivi understood this. Sabu was jumping high for 7 minutes and he was practically sweating…

Vivi : "Stop. Sabu…press the button 13. It will show the pulse rate and heart beat..". Sabu presses no.13. A colorful display comes in the watch.

Pulse rate	:	92/sec
Heart beat	:	Above normal
Suggestion	:	Relax immediately for 7 minutes. Breathe deeply.

After 7 minutes of relaxing and deep breathing Sabu presses the button again.

Pulse rate	:	73/sec
Heart beat	:	PERFECT.

Sabu humps! Shouts!! "Oh! Aha…!". In the mean time Vivi goes quickly to read the manual and she finishes it fast. She has a brilliant mind. She understands anything fast. She is exclaimed with joy…

"Sabu…It is ALL-in-ALL Watch!"

Sabu questions her…." ALL-in-ALL watch means …what it is?" Vivi explains :

" Sabu…It is like…it is like a no it is not comparable. It is just a Clinical Lab in the form of wrist watch. If we wear it and press corresponding buttons we will come to know about our Body temperature, blood sugar levels, ECG, EEG, Pulse Rate, Cholesterol level, Platelets counts in blood, and kidney examination and digestion analysis…and everything…See...You just press button 06…it will show how is your digestion goes on…come on press 06." Sabu presses 06 and the watch displays :

Digestion	:	Very Smooth
Suggestion	:	Can eat snacks and have a cup of Tea.

Sabu in all excitement :

"Vivi...I have not seen a gadget like this. This is tremendous. It not only gives the result but also gives the suggestions...O! Beautiful!! Brilliant Product!!!"

Vivi replies :

"You see there is night suggestion facility. If you press the key 04...you will get suggestion for the night...Shall we try...okay...first myself..."

Vivi presses 04 and there is a display in the watch.

Dinner : Light Tiffin recommended with a cup of Milk.

Suggestion : Go to bed around 22.00 hours.

Vivi : "Sabu...come on you press...". Sabu presses and the display is...

Dinner : Anything you like

Suggestion : Go to bed around 22.00 hours. He again presses the key04.

GOOD NIGHT.

HAVE A GOOD SLEEP!

09. Sabu Birthday

September 29th. 2116.

Yes…It is Sabu's Birth Day!

All the family members Sri, Ben, and Vivi have taken leave to celebrate Sabu's Birth Day. It is morning 10 A.M… Terrace of Shastha apartments. Plastic roof is erected to avoid Sun rays and rain, if so any. There are about 100 chairs. Sabu's friends are the main guests. Other than them we have Vivi's close friends too. Also, we have friends of Sri and Ben. A huge White Vanilla Cake welcomes all. Sabu addresses :

"Okay…good morning all of you. Thanks for your gracious presence and now I am going to cut the cake…"

The crowd : "Hey…Hey…Hey…!"

"Happy Birth day to you…

Happy Birth day to you…

Happy Birth day to ….SSABHU…".

All sang clapping their hands and it was nice to hear the chorus. Sabu cuts the cake. Everyone was waiting to see …to whom the first piece of Cake will go…and everyone is excited. Sabu calmly with a gentle hand-shake gives the First piece to his sister…Vivi. Next to Ben and then to Sri. Then he distributes to everyone.

Sabu also distributes the energy drink ALLVITTA to all and every-one was enjoying the moment. Everyone interacted with the other and rejoiced and shared everything among them Just an Hour. Celebration over. Sabu and family return to the flat 007. Ben calls Vivi and Sabu and tells :

"See…today is Birth Day of Sabu…so myself and Sri are going to gift…a very special gift to both of you…"

"Hey…Hey!!" (Both shout)

"What is it MUM?"

"A SURPRISE!"

"What is the surprise…what is the suspense?" (Sabu)

Ben : " No..No…you can come and see!"

Sabu : "We are going out…Where Ma?"

Ben : "Suspense!"

After 15 minutes…Sri, Ben, Vivi and Sabu get in to a Navan Jeep and it starts moving through the outskirts of CHEN.

Jeep stops.

I.S.R.O. GADHET MALL!

Ooo! It is a Big mall. It is 7 storey building. Sabu and Vivi are first time visitors to this mall. So there is excitement with joy. To some extent they are even shocked!

All of them use the Elevator and each the 4th floor. A BIG SHOW ROOM!!

'KALA YANTRA'….It is the name of the shop. All enter in to it. And Sabu with astonishment asks his Mum :

"Mum…what is 'Kala Yantra'? What does it mean?"

"Dear son…it means…in Samskrit it is TIME MACHINE!"

Sabu : "What…a Time Machine?"

Vivi : "What is that?"

———◆———

10. 7 O' 7!

Sri introduces his kids to the Special Officer of ISRO. He is the in-charge for 'Kala Yantra'…i.e…..Time Machine. His name is Viji. He is young Space Scientist of ISRO.

Sri :"Mr.Viji…this is my daughter Vivi aged 13 and this is my son Sabu aged

9…Both have got ISRO Award for Junior Scientists…Ne and my wife Ben have an appointment with the Chief of ISRO. It will take an hour …I think…Mean time…You please explain about this Time Machine to them. Actually I am going to purchase it and the Chief Okayed my proposal in writing. So we will leave…you please take care of them…"

Viji : "Sure Sir…I will update your kids about the 7 O' 7…the Time Machine…"

Sri and Ben leave the Place. Viji offers the kids a seat to sit.

Viji : "Have you ever heard of Time Machine? Time Travel?"

Vivi : "I have read a Novel about that…"

Sabu : "I knew something"

Viji : "What is that something?"

Sabu : "Sir…It is travelling to some place which is in the past…"

Viji : "Ya…very good. First I will tell you one thing. Your parents are the First persons to buy this Time Machine…7 O' 7! It costs 7 crore points. That is if you have a WC*5 , almost a year's salary will be deducted. It is such a costly Machine…"

Sabu : " O! My goodness…7 Crores…mmm…"

Vivi : "Who manufactured this one?"

Viji : "It is indigenously built. That is it is totally manufactured in Nava Bharath. And it is the first product of this kind in the world itself. It took almost 22 years to build it. Your parents have purchased it for you. You lucky kids…you must know that only 2 persons can travel in this Time machine…"

Sabu : "Sir…please tell us about its properties and functioning…"

Viji : "Good. Very good. No test drive is possible. If you once start the Machine it will run for 28 days only…remember only 28 days it will work and automatically it will expire."

Sabu : "Just 28 days…?"

Viji : " Yes…you must reach your starting point before the 29th day… that is to your residence. If you did not reach back in 28 days you will VANISH in Space. Mind that you can travel only 28 days. This is the most important point."

Viji opens the door of Time machine.

7 O' 7

It is in Tri-Color. (Old Indian Flag which is in use now also)
Saffron!

White!!

Green!!!

And in the white portion you have 24 Blue color diameters or straight lines in Blue color which denotes the Dharma Chakra. Vivi and Sabu get in to 7 O' 7 and peep to the machine.

Viji : "Yes…Sabu and Vivi…you have Star shaped meters in this Machine…as you have round or circle shaped meters in a car or jeep. The Red Star shows the speed. You can accelerate speed as you wish. But there is a precaution to be noted. You can accelerate to the maximum the speed of the light. Do you know the speed of light?"

Sabu : "Yes sir…It is 1, 86,000 kilometers/second"

Viji   : "Yes…Exactly. And that is your limit."

Sabu : "If we accelerate more than that what will happen?"

Viji : "Very important. No one knows what will happen. We are not sure. We know nothing about it. It is still a mystery. May be that you land in some star or planet or vanish to dust. Or you may enter some place beyond our Galaxy…the Milky Way… no one knows what will happen…"

Vivi : "So…for what it has been built?"

Viji : "Ya…I will come to the point…you can travel to any TIME in the PAST and stay there for not more than 48 hours. You have to re-enter the machine within 48 hours. This is a moot point. Understand…?"

Sabu : "Awesome!"

Vivi : "Beauty!"

Viji : "You have 2 modes....1...visible mode and 2 the invisible mode...

Visible mode means you will be visible to the characters of the past...and invisible means you cannot be seen by the characters anyhow. If you select the visible mode you can interact with the members of the past...but one condition YOU CANNOT change the HISTORY. Are You clear?"

Sabu and Vivi : "Yes...sir....very clear..."

Viji : "you can use this machine as a Helicopter within the Blue Planet (Earth) as many times as you wish....No conditions....but if you travel to the past..Say 1857...you can travel to the point only once. And you can stay up to 48 hours only and you should return to the machine within 48 hours. Please note this carefully to avoid a TIME ACCIDENT. If you miss the time ...that's all. You will vanish in Time and Space. There will be no way to reach back to your home. This you must know... Can you catch my point?"

Sabu : "Sure, Sir....It is great!" Vivi : "Yes...I understood the importance of TIME"

Viji : "See...you can visit B.C. or A.D....accordingly pressing the 'HALA' button...i.e.....Time button...which is in yellow in color. Yes you can select the time by typing the number on it. You have a virtual keyboard at the bottom...You can there select the PLACE you want.

SEE...YOU ARE THE FIRSTHUMANS TO TRAVEL TIME.

Since both f your parents are Staff of ISRO…and also you both have been awarded the JUNIOR SCIENTISTS of ISRO you have got this opportunity ..

First…

First in Human History…

First 2 people to travel TIME!!!"

Sabu : "We are the luckiest!"

Vivi : "Ya…we are gifted!"

Viji : "Ya…sure. I will give you 2 copies of this manual…I mean… this Machine's manual. Read it carefully. Understand it. And that's the key. Use it! Experience it!! Share it with the world!!! It is you both have huge responsibility to let others know your experiences for 28 days…All the Best. Have the Keys and Remote Control…And Very All the BEST!"

Sabu : "Thank you Sir…We will do our best!"

Vivi : "I too assure you that, Sir."

Viji : "Yes…you have the 7 O' 7….All the BEST."

11. Getting Ready

7 O' 7

It is in the terrace of Shastha apartments. It needs only 10 x10 square feet space. Sri, Ben, Vivi and Sabu are all taking Lemon Tea and discussing about the 7 O' 7 travel.

Ben : "Have you both read the manuals?"

Sabu : "Yes…Mum…We are thorough in it."

Sri : "See…Sabu and Vivi your travel is its first of its kind in the human history. Your travel and your experiences will be registered and all your sayings will be written in a Time Capsule and it will be buried in the Earth… Humans even after millions of years will have an access to your Time Capsule and will be directly come to know your words… Is that clear?"

Vivi : "Yes…Dad..We know what we are going to do…"

Ben : "Be calm and composed. Do not get excited. Do not get in to anxiety. Take all the precautions that are needed…Have nice 28 days. Remember the 29th day you must be back here. Never forget this. Okay?"

Sabu : "Okay mum…Sure. Done."

Vivi : Dear Mum and Dad, myself and Sabu are really very lucky. We know that we are the first humans to undergo Time Travel. It is a great opportunity. Really we will grab it. Do not worry about us. We will take all the precautions that is needed and will travel with ease and comfort. We will plan everything. Nothing to worry."

Ben : "That's good. All the best."

Sabu : "Dad only one question…We may need to meet Mr.Viji the special Officer of ISRO in between our travel. Is it possible?"

Sri : "For what?"

Sabu : " We want to discuss certain facts."

Sri : "okay….you can visit him whenever you feel doing so…no problem. Okay…kids tomorrow you are starting your travel… okay?"

Ben : "Take enough food and drinks …okay?"

Sabu : "Yes, Mum…Sure." Sri and Ben leave the place.

Sabu : "hey…Vivi…Have decided about our first travel…I mean whom to meet at first?"

Vivi : "I was thinking for the past couple of days about that and I selected one person!"

Sabu : "Who is that?"

Vivi : "What about you? You did not think on that line?"

Sabu : " I also thought and selected person"

Vivi : "Oh! Really great…Who is that person?"

Sabu comes closer to Vivi and whispers the name.

Vivi : " Oh! My goodness…We both have selected the same person…
It is really great. Two parallel lines meet at infinity. It is like
that. Ya…I also selected him only.

Sabu : "Really…it is amazing! We have the same thought wave
notion. It is a good sign to our start."

Vivi : "So tomorrow we will meet…."

Sabu : "O! Oh! The GREAT….."

12. The Great (Dictator)......
Actor!

E_Z...

EZZ...

EZZZZZZZZZZZZ!!!

7 O' 7 take off. Start. 3...2...1...EZZZZZZZZZZZ!!!

Sabu : "Vivi...Press A.D. button!"

Vivi : "Done!"

Sabu : "Press A.D. and type 1940..."

Vivi : "Done!"

Sabu : "See the right meter...it asks the location...type the Great Dictator Shooting spot..."

Vivi does it. And they start. The Great Dictator Shooting spot.

7 O' 7 flies. EZZZZZZZZZZZZZZ....EEEZZZZZZZ ZZZZZZ ZZZZ....

Sabu : "What an experience?"

Vivi : "It is awesome!"

Sabu : "Hey…We do not feel time…isn't it?" "See...The Earth clock…"

Vivi : "Hey…we have travelled 13 hours…"

Sabu : "Oh! Hey…it is great!"."Hey…see the output meter…We have only few seconds for destination".

7

6

5

4

3

2

1

The grounds. The Great Dictator Shooting spot. 7 O' 7 lands smoothly at the one end of the corner of the huge grounds. The shooting is going on. There are 1000s of soldiers standing at ease. There is a stage.

Hey!

There is Chaplin!!

He is in Hitler get up!!!

Shooting is going on. The climax of the movie. Sabu and Vivi record all the audio and video. They are near…nut out of the shooting field.

Chaplin : "Lights…Camera…Action". Camera rolling. Chaplin in Hitler get up gets emotional and in a soft but determined voice….

" I am sorry, but I do not want to be an emperor. That is not my business. I do not want to rule or conquer anyone. I should like to help everyone-if possible-Jew<Gentile Blackman-White. We all want to help one another. Human beings are like that. We want to live by each other's happiness-not by each other's misery. We do not want to hate any despise one another. In this world there is a room for everyone. And the good earth is rich and can provide for everyone. The way of life can be free and beautiful, but we have lost the way…"

Sabu : "Hey…he is emotional and taking this scene at a stretch…"

Vivi : "Ya…he is simply great…See there are people with tears in their eyes…"

Sabu : "Ya…I am shooting everything…"

Chaplin continues…

"Greed has poisoned men's souls, has barricaded the world with hate, and has goose-stepped us in to misery and bloodshed. We have developed speed, but we have shut ourselves in. Machinery that gives abundance has left us in want. Our knowledge has made us cynical. Our cleverness hard and unkind. WE THINK TOO MUCH AND FEEL TOO LITTLE. NORE THAN MACHINERY WE NEED HUMANITY. MORE THAN CLEVERNESS WE NEED KINDNESS ABD GENTLENESS. Without those qualities life will be violent and all will be lost…

The aero plane and radio have brought us closer together..The very nature of inventions cries out for goodness in man-cries out of Universal Brotherhood-for the unity of us all. Even now my voice is reading millions throughout the world-millions of despairing man, woman and little children-victims of a system that makes men torture and imprison innocent people.

To those who can hear me, I say-do not despair. The misery that is now upon is but the passing of the greed-the bitterness of men who fear the way of human progress. The hate of man will pass, and dictators die, and the power they took from the people will return to the people. And so long as man die, liberty will never perish...

Soldiers!

Do not give yourselves to brutes-men who despise you-enslave you-who regiment your lives-tell you what to do- what to think and what to feel! Who drill you-diet you-treat you like cattle, use you as cannon folder. Do not give yourselves to these unnatural men-machine men with machine minds and machine hearts! YOU ARE NOT MACHINES! YOU ARE NOT CATTLE! YOU ARE MEN! You have to love humanity in hearts. You do not hate! Only the unloved hate-the unloved and unnatural!

Soldiers! Do not fight for slavery! Fight for Liberty!!

Sabu : "What an emotional speech!'

Vivi : With tears, "He is just great!" "Wait let him finish the Shot..."

...Chaplin continues...

Dictators free themselves but they enslave the people! Now let us fight to fulfill that promise! Let us fight to free the world-to do away with national barriers-to do away with greed, with hate and intolerance. Let us fight for a world of reason, a world where science and progress will lead to all men's happiness.

Soldiers!

In the name of Democracy, let us all unite!"

Cut! Cut!!

Shot okay.

Charlie sits in the Director's chair. Sabu and Vivi enter the place.

Vivi : "He is my brother Sabu and I am Vivi. We are from Blue planet and in to the Kepler Planet…

Charlie : "O! My kids! Welcome. What can I do for you?"

Sabu : "Only a few questions…You have to answer them. Are You a Communist?"

Charlie : "I am for the people. If you call me a Communist…I do not mind."

Vivi : "Sir…in Your Modern Times movie you have totally criticized the Capitalist system and you have raised your voice in support of all the workers…"

Charlie : "Ya. That is the truth. I speak and act only for the truth."

Sabu : "Sir…well said. Sir…Our time is getting to the close…ewe enjoyed your acting and direction abilities…one last question…what is your purpose of taking movies?"

Charlie : "it is open secret. I will whisper in your ears,"

Charlie gets hold of Sabu and Vivi and whisper for few seconds.

Charlie : " BYE…BYE…!"

Sabu and Vivi enter 7 O' 7 after 47 hours. Almost very close.

7 O' 7!

EEZZZZZZZZZZZZZZZZZZZZZZZZZZ!!

Take off!!!

Vivi : "Did you record the whispering of Chaplin?"

Sabu : "Sure. Then What?"

Vivi : "Okay…put the chip in the Visual Box. And make his whispering to a Audio-Visual mode…"

Sabu : "Okay…now in 3 seconds you will see and hear his voice in this player…."

Vivi : "3…2…1…0"

MAKE PEOPLE LAUGH!

MAKE PEOPLE THINK!!

MAKE PEOPLE HAPPY!!!

ACT FOR GLOBAL PEACE!!!!3

13. The Great Pyramids

7 O' 7

EEEZZZZZZZZZZZZZZZZZZZ!!!

Year : 2713 B.C.

Location : the Great Pyramid construction site

Speed : Normal

Mode : Visible

Everything operated via a Remote control. 7 O' 7 lands at the construction site of Great pyramids of Khufu, the Egypt. It is really unbelievable! Millions of Workers are working in the site. Vivi and Sabu are astonished totally. The Pyramid is 3/4th completed. Workers are dragging the large giant size stones with the help of wooden logs and pulleys. What a tremendous sight to view this massive work. The Great Pyramids of Khufu is one of the Wonders of Ancient World, which is still alive. What is pyramid? It is squire at the base. And there are 4 tri-angles being the surfaces which converge at a top point. This is Geometric basis. The Great Pyramid is built of lime stones and real granite blocks. It is an architectural master piece! The blocks weighing from 2.5 tons to 15 tons are used to build. You know how many blocks are used for this purpose? Oh! 2, 00,000 blocks. Vivi and Sabu after astonishment enter the building site.

Vivi : "Have you taken the Translator Box?"

Sabu : "Ya…I have." They go near the common workers who were dragging the granite stones.

Vivi : "Hello! Gentlemen…We are from Blue planet…we want to talk to you about this wonderful master piece…the pyramids…"

Sabu operates the Translator Box and presses the button Egyptian-English. What Vivi spoke got translated and the box said the same thing in Egyptian. The two workers got frightened hearing the Egyptian voice.

"What is this?". They wondered in Egyptian.

Sabu : "Gentlemen… do not worry…this is just a automatic mechanical device which is used for translating …". It also got translated. The 2 workers came to consciousness and were able to digest the Translator Box. One of the man asked in Egyptian and the box translated…

"Who are YOU?".

Vivi : "We are from Blue planet. And we want to know more about these pyramids?". And the workers spoke something and it was immediately translated by the Box.

"We are just workers. We carry out the commands of our Chief. We do not know anything about these Pyramids. We think it symbolizes our Sun God RA and its rays…We do not know anything else…Our religious chief and the architect commands millions of workers and we do what he says …"

"Who is he?". At once translated. And there comes the reply.

"IMHOTEP…you can meet him…See there he is…". He points at a distance. Sabu and Vivi slowly walk towards the Imhotep and used the Translator Box to the astonishment of Imhotep. After few minutes the Dialogue which was translated was"

"Why do you want know about Pyramids?"

"It is one of the wonders of the world even after 4000 years…"

"Yes."

"What is the specialty about this?"

"It is Grand Pyramid of Khufu…Egypt. It spreads to 13 acres. It has a height of 147 meters; the angle of inclination of 4 tri-angles is 52 degrees. This is Tomb. This is for Pharaohs. Mainly father of all Pharaohs…I mean the Sun god…That's all I can reveal…okay?"

"Who decides the dimensions and on what principle he decides that?"

"Sorry kids…It's myself…Imhotep who decides everything which is revealed to me by my God."

"WHO IS YOUR God?"

"The SUN…"

" Cannot you explain further?"

"No kids…It is a Religious secret. The pyramid which is great will be a wonder for many centuries and anyone can explore the secret behind these dimensions…"

"What is the secret?"

" I can not reveal. But one thing I can tell you is that in future say about 4000 or 5000 years from now….a Mathematical Genius would decipher all the secrets of these pyramids…So you can leave this place. I have tremendous work to carry on…"

Vivi : "Okay…Imhotep …all the best…your work is Fantastic and Fabulous"

Imhotep : "The secrets will be deciphered…Bye…bye…"

BYE.

Vivi and Sabu reach 7 O' 7.

7…6…5…4…3…2…1…

EEE EEEZZZZZZZZZZZZZZZZZZZZ

ZZZZZZZZ!!!!!!!!!!!!!!!!!!!!!!!!!!!!

14. The most unfortunate Scientist!

Posthumously declared Father of Genetics!!

7 O' 7

Sabu : "Vivi...we will meet Gregor Mendel the Great Scientist next..."

Vivi : "I too thought on the same line..."

Sabu : "His theory was Re-Discovered in 1900 only, that is after 30 years of his demise."

Vivi : "Ya...he was the most Unfortunate Scientist in the history."

Sabu : "But the TRUTH triumphed at last..."

Vivi : "What is the use Sabu?...Mendel in his life time was not at all recognized. He was treated as if he was a great fool!"

Sabu : "Ya...but NOW the world claims that he is the Father of Modern Genetics! : "

Vivi : "When did he die?"

Sabu : " 6th January, 1884…"

Vivi : "When did he submit his thesis?"

Sabu : " 1865 and 1866"

Vivi : "He died in 1884…almost 18 years after publishing his theory…O! My goodness…I am not able to digest this…"

Sabu : "Ya…Vivi…ne too!"

Vivi : "Location?"

Sabu : "Pea garden of Mendel in the Church. Visible mode"

7

6

5

4

3

2

1

EEEEEEEEEEEZZZZZZZZZZZZZZZZZZZZZZZZZ!!!

Pea Garden in the Church. Mendel is watering the plants. Vivi and Sabu enter the scene.

Vivi : "Hello…Mr. Mendel…"

Mendel : "Did you call me mental?"

Vivi : "No sir…I said Mr. Mendel…"

Sabu : "What are you doing, sir?"

Vivi : "We are proud to talk to you, Sir."

Mendel : "I am watering my Pea plants. That's all."

Sabu : "You are a great Scientist…Sir…"

Mend : "Who said so?"

Vivi : "Okay Sir…You were doing Pea-Plant experiment for Plant hybridization for almost 7 years from 1856 to 1863. Is not it?"

Mend : "Yes…so what?"

Sabu : "What is your major finding…Please explain in detail…sir."

Mend : "I gave 3 most important laws in the field of Botany… Yes…1. Law of Segregation 2. Law of independent assortment and 3. Law of Dominance."

Vivi : "Yes Sir…really great!"

Sabu : "You conceived the idea of heredity units, which you called 'Factors'!(After 30 years these 'factors' were named as GENES! And Mendel was Called Father of Modern Genetics…most importantly after his demise! What a Treatment to a Genius!)"

Vivi : "Sir…when did you publish your theory of inheritance?"

Mend : "Oh! Aha!! No… I am trying to forget it…but I remember it was 1865 and 1866…I published."

Sabu : "What was the reaction of the world?."

Mend : "Oh...Unbearable!! The scientists of the world called me a fool!."

Vivi : "Why?."

Mend : "I was the first scientist to use Mathematics and Statistics to the field of Botany."

Sabu : "Really great!"

Mend : "No use...all scientists and the scientific world called me a fool and mad!."

Vivi : "It is really surprising....Mathematics is the Mother of all Sciences. To apply that to Botany was really a superb great thing...I do not know why rehected this..."

Mend : "Only future has to prove my theory was right...I did pea-plant experiments for almost 7 years...and these pea-plants were the basis for my Research and fining the laws of Inheritance..."

Sabu : "I really feel sorry for you, Sir..."

Mend : "What can you do? I am totally depressed and surrendered myself to the Almighty and I want to die...'Pea'ce fully!"

Sabu : "Peas Fully?"

Mend : "Hey...you are sharp, I say...I have become a MONK...No more Science. No more laws...No more Research...Only watering the Pea-plants and I never think about anything now. I pray to God a peaceful death."

Vivi : " Sir, We feel very sorry for you. I assure you in 30 years your Theory will be accepted by the world and you will be named the Father of Modern Genetics….What you called as 'factors' will be named as 'GENES'…and you will really receive the recognition. That's sure."

Mend : "Who wants it? Who want a Posthumous award?."

Sabu : "Sorry Sir…we can do nothing. But we understand your theory and feelings…"

Vivi : " Sir…If the Re-Birth theory is TRUTH…certainly you will be born again as a Scientist and you will be rewarded in your life time itself…Okay, Sir…we are moving."

Mend : "Thank you kids…Bye."

7 O' 7

5

4

3

2

1

EZZZZZZZZZZZZZZZZZZZZZZZZZZZZZZ!!!!!!!!!!!!

15. The Greatest Revolutionary!

Year : 1923 A.D.

Location : Soviet Union….Lenin's office

3…2…1…EEZZZZZZZZZZ!

Vivi and Sabu enter Lenin's Office. Lenin was writing something. Above him there were Karl Marx and Engels Photos. His office was full of book shelves. He has 1000s of books around him. He was keen on writing.

Sabu : "Excuse me, sir.."

Lenin : "Yes…come in. Take your seats." Sabu and Vivi sit before Lenin.

Vivi : "Sir…we are coming from Blue planet…"

Lenin : "O! That's good."

Sabu : "We just want to chat with you and ask some questions."

Lenin : "Sure…Carry on."

Vivi : "You once said 'the goal of Socialism is Communism'…What is that? Can you elaborate?"

Lenin : "Yes…it is true. But it cannot be explained in just a few words.…It is impossible to predict the TIME and PROGRESS of REVOLUTION. It is governed by more or less mysterious laws."

Sabu : "Not clear, Sir."

Lenin : "Okay I will put it simply. State owned property is Socialism. All are equals. All will be paid accordingly. This is Socialism. But what is the goal of Socialism? It is nothing but Communism! I do not know or I cannot predict when will Communism will come in to force…Simply…it is a State without State. People rule themselves.

Vivi : "NO Government?"

Lenin : "yes…the stage Communism will wither away all form of State and Policing. No one to rule. People rule themselves. There will be no private property. I mean there will be a Private Spectacles…but not a Spectacle producing unit. It would be Commune based.

Sabu : "What about the worker's condition?"

Lenin : "All people will work. Each according to his ABILITY…And more importantly they will be paid what they NEED. One will get all his needs."

Vivi : "There will be no rulers and people get what they want. Isn't it?"

Lenin : "Yes...Nations wither their boundaries. And all state forums will wither away...and a state-less world or Global Commune with high standards will emerge."

Sabu : "Okay...people work and they get what they need. Is that alone is Communism?"

Lenin : "No...No...Certainly not. It is a ocean. I told you only one drop...But I can emphasize one thing. Humans will develop all branches of Sciences and there will be a Great Revolution in Science, Technology and RE-SEARCH. All humans will start exploring the space! Yes...humans will work to understand Nature completely and change the situations to their benefits.'

Vivi : "YOU mean..."

Lenin "People will fight against Nature and establish a Heaven in the world! Shortly it would happen...and that is Communism."

Sabu : "So you emphasize that political and Scientific Revolution will be the future..."

Lenin : "Certainly...Revolution means 'Change'. We need a change in our political system. We need Socialism! And then a Change in Scientific outlook and RESEARCH!! We must explore our Galaxy, the Milky Way. Only when people are self-sustained and have free time to think and act...The Greatest Scientific Revolution will occur. That's why I told you that the goal of Socialism is nothing but Communism."

Sabu : "Is it possible at one stroke?"

Lenin : "Why not? People should acquire power. People should dictate everything. Class-caste-gender-color-ethnic-linguistic differences will slowly wither away.

One Globe!

One Commune!!

One Culture!!!

Sabu : " How is that possible, Sir?"

Lenin : "The history of all countries shows that the working class exclusively by its own efforts is able to develop Trade-Union consciousness. We the leaders and Revolutionaries should make then 'Political' and 'National' Conscious. We should develop the working class to a new Socially-Conscious people. Yes… we the Revolutionaries are the Catalysts…people when freed from economic burden will create Heaven in the Earth!

Lon Live Communism!

Sabu : "Thank you…Sir."

Vivi : "Our Revolutionary Greetings to you…Comrade."

Lenin : "Same to You."

7 O' 7

4

3

2

1

EZZZZZZZZZZZZ !!!

16. The Patriotic Saint

5

4

3

2

1

EEEEEEEEEEEEZZZZZZZZ ZZZZZZZZZZZZZZZZ!!!

1901 A.D.

Location : Ramakrishna Math, Belur, Bengal, India.

Mode   : Visible

Vivi and Sabu enter the Math. Vivekananda was writing something. He was in Saffron clothing. His face was clear and bright. He had very sharp eyes. His physique was gigantic.

Sabu : "Excuse me Ji…Namesthe."

Vivek : "Come in…Take your seat."

Vivi : "we are coming from Blue planet and we are totally inclined to you and your ideas. We want to chat with you…"

Vivek : "About what?"

Sabu : "Ji…about Education system…"

Vivek : "O! My God…you can ask your questions…"

Vivi : "What is Education?"

Vivek : "What is education? Is it book learning? No. Is it diverse knowledge? Not even that. The training by which the current and expression of will that are brought under control and become fruitful is called Education." He continues :

"The education you are getting (19th and 20th century) now has some good points. But it has a tremendous disadvantage which is so great that the good things are weighed down. In the first place it is not man making education, it is merely and entirely a negative education. A negative education or any training based on negation is worse than death. The child is taken to school and the first thing he learns is that his father is a fool, the second thing is that his grandfather is lunatic, and the third thing is that all his teachers are hypocrites, the fourth all the sacred books are mere lies! By the time he is a man of negation, kifeless and boneless. And the result is that fully 50 years of such education has not produced one Original in the 3 presidencies…

Vivi : "So…what do you say about real education?"

Vivek : "Education is not filling the minds with lots of facts. Perfecting the instrument and getting complete mastery of my own mind is the ideal of education. Education is the manifestation of perfection already that exists in man.

If education is identical with information, the libraries are the greatest sages in the world and encyclopedia are the Rishis!

Sabu : "Okay…Ji…what do you think about secrets of life about?"

Vivek : "…life is a series of fights and disillusionments…the secret of life is not enjoyment but education through experience. But alas, we are called off the moment we really begin to learn. That seems to be a potent argument for future existence…

That man or Society which has nothing to learn is already in the jaws of death.

Vivi : "What should be ideal of education?"

Vivek : "The education which does not help the common masses of people to equip themselves for the struggle of life. Which does not bring out the strength of character, a spirit of Philanthropy, and the courage of a Lion-is it worth of the name? Real education is that which enables one to stand on one's own legs.

The ideal of education, all training should be this man-making. But instead of that, we are always trying to polish up the outside. What is the use of polishing outside, when there is nothing inside? The end and aim of all training is to make the man grow. The first duty is to educate the people. If the mountain does not come to Mohammed, Mohammed must go to mountain! If the poor cannot come to education, education must reach them at Plough, in factory everywhere… If the poor boy cannot come to education then education should go to him.

Vivi : "Nice…very nice JI…"

Sabu : "What is to be done..Ji?"

Vivek : "All the wealth of the world cannot help one little Indian Village if the people are not taught to help themselves. Our work should be mainly educational, both MORAL and INTELLECTUAL.

Educate and raise the masses! Then alone a Nation is possible!!

Education, education and education alone!

Travelling through the many cities of Europe and observing in then the comforts and education of even the poor people, there was brought to mu mind the state of our own people...I have shed tears for the pity Indians.

Vivi : "It was a pleasure to talk to you, Ji. I remember in 1893 at Chicago you started your oration with 'Brothers and Sisters of America...!' and whole audience stood up and applauded for several minutes. And you gave the historical speech in the World Parliament of Religions...the speech was simply superb. You brought back the glory of India and Indian people back fantastically..."

Sabu : "Really you have done an excellent job, Ji. We will leave now."

Vivi : "All the best to your Ramakrishna Math!"

Vivek : "Om Shanthi! Shanthi!! Shanthi!!!

(NOTE : The Birth day of Swami Vivekananda that is 12th January is celebrated as the NATIONAL YOUTH DAY throughout India and now in Nava Bharath.

Let us salute the Patriotic Saint!)

17. Great Primitive Commune!

Vivi : "Sabu…we have almost persons of different times…and all about them…we have read and seen in the movies…"

Sabu : "Ya…Vivi…We have travelled very backwards…Vivi we have a unknown history of Vedic Age…"

Vivi : "Yes some say it is 3000 years B.C. and some say it is 5000 or 7000 years B.C."

Sabu : "According to history it is Iron Age or Stone Age…people lived in Clans and they were tribes…isn't it?"

Vivi : "Yes…they were cannibals in the old age. We must be careful."

Sabu : "okay…this will be adventurous travel…Let us select the INVISIBLE mode…so that no one can see us."

Vivi : "Ya…that precaution is absolutely needed."

Sabu : "Okay…which year to select…Shall I select randomly…say 3…4…5…6…, is it okay?"

Vivi : "Ya…come on press B.C. first…"

Sabu : "Done!"

Vivi : "Enter the year 3456!"

Sabu : "Yes we are going to 3456 B.C….that is almost 5000 years
           ago…"

Vivi : "I am little scared…"

Sabu : "Do not worry. We have selected invisible mode…isn't it?"

Vivi : "Location"

Sabu : "Type Indus Valley…"

Vivi : "Done."

    4

    3

    2

    1

EEEEEEEEZZZZZZZZZZZZZZZZZZZZZ !!!!!!!!!!!!!!!!!!!!!!!!
!!!!!!!!!!!!!!!

3456 B.C.???

Sabu and Vivi are shocked!!! ???

Along the riverside there are beautiful

Small huts. They have used bam boos and

Coconut Tree leaves to build it.

It is well planned huts.

Totally astonished.

Sabu : " Wav…" great !.

Vivi : " Ya.. they are civilized "

Sabu : " See these …. fields…"

Vivi : Ya… Paddy fields."

Sabu : They know agriculture too! "

Vivi : Really great !"

Sabu : "See more than to people go to the fields with plough!"

Vivi : " Ya.. Its made of iron"

Sabu : " See… something like a board is there in the fields…"

Vivi : " Ya…. take a snap and get it translated to English …..quick…."

Sabu : It is Jana Bhoomi!

Vivi : What's the translation…………?

Sabu : "It means Peoples land"

Vivi : "Sabu … this is great. No private ownership of land. It is all owned by people

Something like a communist society…."

Sabu : "See at the right… There are hundreds of cows , bulls and goats maizing the grasslands…. It's also owned by the clan itself.

Vivi : " See…there are no cattle in individual huts…. All the cattle are in a common place………which mean the people, clan own all the cattle".

Sabu : "Great !"

Vivi : " You noticed one thing…… this is morning all men go out….. Some to paddy Fields and some for hunting…"

Sabu : " Ya…. They wear animal skins as their dresses………..Oh! Vivi see there is a big stone carved as a cow!"

Vivi : I think they worship cow. And I hope they have banned cow slaughter!"

Sabu : "Why?"

Vivi : "Hey…think like this. The cow gives milk, ghee, butter, butter milk and curd. It gives everything to us without any expectations…even after its death its skin is used to make drums and preparing coats to all…It is unselfish and benevolent."

Sabu : "Ya…Ya…That's why they have banned cow slaughter…and Vivi you noticed one thing…there is huge funnel like apparatus at every hut."

Vivi : "Ya…See smoke is coming out."

Sabu : "Yes…women are cooking inside…and see some women work with the cattle."

Vivi : " It is great…They know FIRE!"

Sabu : "How come?"

Vivi : "They must have invented it."

Sabu : " See a man from forest comes in a Chariot with full of Jack fruits!"

Vivi : "Hey…Great…they have already had invented the wheels…. Superb!"

Sabu : "Amazing! Splendid!! Fabulous!!!"

Vivi : "Yes…there is a division of Labor too…Men go for hunting and agriculture. Women take care of cooking and the Cattle."

Sabu : "They cook and eat! What a Surprise!"

Vivi : "Let us go near the banyan Tree…"

Sabu : "Hey…one old man with a long beard is writing something… actually carving in the palm leaves.."

Vivi : "Yes…the Vedic people are educated and know to read and write…"

Sabu ; "Yes…their language is Samskrit."

Vivi : "We must have selected the visible mode….Then we would have interacted with them…Hey…see children are going to the big hut…The oldman gets in…Yes…let us record the conversation and we have spent more than 40 hours looking the Vedic commune! Fantastic!!.'

Sabu : "Let us go near the big hut."

The old man says…"Namesthe. Subha Saya"

Vivi : "Sabu…put the recorder to Display Text Mode and get it translated."

Sabu : "It is salutations and well wishes greetings;"

Vivi : "Ooo! It is a School."

Sabu : "Ya."

The old man with the long beard says "Nathi katcha. Gayathri Manthra Vathathu. Dhyananam Karothi. "

Vivi : "What is it? Get the text displayed…"

GO TO RIVERSIDE.

TELL THE GAYATHRI MANTHRA.

AND MEDITATE.

All the children go to river bank. They invariably look at the Sun. All in Chorus chant…

OM.

Bhur Bhuvasa

Thathsaverineyam

Bargothevasya-theemaghee

Thyooyona Prachathoyadth.

Vivi : It is very pleasant to hear. Though we did not understand the meaning…it is very pleasant to hear itself…Very commending…I think they are worshipping the Sun…Okay...Sabu see the Text of the Manthra…."

Om!

O! Almighty Light!

You are responsible for the all the intellect on Earth

I bow you. Please ignite my intellect in the right direction

Bless with the good intellect. I meditate upon you!

Vivi : "O! beautiful...there is no mention about any God or Goddesses. Only the transcended Light is worshipped. The SUN is mediated upon."

Sabu : "This is the Gayathri Manthra. I am sure."

Vivi : "Ya...it is simple and great! The sun is the meditating object. It is too good!"

Sabu : "We are out of Time. We must soon reach 7 O' 7."

Vivi : "Ya...we can go...you noticed one thing. These people are highly literate and civilized...all live in harmony and are happy. No private property. Land and cattle are owned by all that is the clan. And every one takes what he needs ...whether paddy or milk...really great!"

Sabu : "I think this is the society Karl Marx and Engels were talking about!"

Vivi : "Yes. Sure. 100% sure. This is the Primitive Commune Society!"

18. The Sky is not the Limit!

7 O' 7

EZZZZZZZZZZZZZ!

Sabu : "We should do something.."

Vivi : "What something?"

Sabu : "Vivi…we have got a Time Machine. Its duration is almost over. Only a few days are left…before it expires…"

Vivi : "Leaving today…there are only 7 days left…Then the life of 7 O' 7 will vanish…I know that."

Sabu : " Olay…today…we will meet TIMES PERSON OF THE 20th Century…This title was awarded in 1999!"

Vivi : "A right choice! A genius move to meet the Genius. You know he…Albert Einstein was born on 14th March, 1879! What is the beauty of it?"

Sabu : "Oh! Ya… he was born on Mystical Number Pi Day."

Vivi : "yes….Pi=3.14…so 14th of 3rd month that is March 14th is celebrated as Pi Day throughout the world…"

Sabu : "A genius was born on Pi Day. Is that anything to do with him and the date?"

Vivi : "Let us not go in to speculations…you know one thing …'Annus Mirabalis' (Latin Phrase)?"

Sabu : "I have heard…but I forgot."

Vivi : "Annus Mirabalis means 'Wonderful Year' in Latin.

Sabu : "Which year?"

Vivi : "1905! Yes…this is the year Albert Einstein presented all his scientific papers related to Time, Space and Relativity. The equation E=mc2 was also presented in this year only. E stands for energy. 'm' for mass. And 'c' speed of the light. This is the equation that shook the world! Also, hi main theory Photo Electric Effect…first of all proved that 'Light' is not a wave. It is made up of particles and he called it PHOTONS. The speed of light/photons is

1, 80,000kms/sec."

Sabu : "Humma! Humma!! What a speed? Unimaginable…He got his Noble prize for Quantum Physics Theory in 1921!

Vivi : "Enter 1921…"

Sabu : "Done…"

Vivi : "Enter Visible Mode and Location?"

Sabu : "Albert Einstein's residence in America!"

4

3

2

1

EEEEEEEEEEE   *ZZZZZZZZZZZZZZZZZZ*!!!

Einstein : "Come in kids…"

Sabu : "Good afternoon Sir…we are from Blue planet and we want to chat with you for a short time…"

Einstein : "So…you mean to say I am from Kepler planet…okay let us not go into the unwanted details…you can ask your questions, right away."

Vivi : "You are a great genius. You are a great scientist. What do you think about India?"

Einstein : "O! O!! India!!! We owe a lot to Indians, who taught us to count, without which no worthwhile Scientific Discovery could have been made…"

Vivi : "Yes…Sir…You are 100% correct."

Einstein : "Not only that …the language Samskrit contributed by Indians is much great. It is a vibrant language. It is Logical and mere learning the language ignites one's intellect and IQ. I am sure."

Sabu : "Yes sir…It is a Classical language…isn't it? Sir…You proposed Theory of Relativity. You say Time and Space are inseparable and also you say TIME is the 4th dimension. Can you explain it ?"

Einstein : " When you are courting a nice girl an hour seems like a second. When you sit on a red-hot cinder a second seems like an hour. That's the Relativity."

Vivi : "Splendid…Sir."

Einstein : "A clever person solves the problem. A wise person avoids it…See…Science without religion is lame, religion without Science is blind. Also, Reality is a mere illusion, albeit a very persistent one. I have no special talents. I am only passion-ately curious."

Sabu : "Splendid…genius words…what do you think as important?"

Einstein : "the important thing is not stop questioning. Curiosity has its own reasons for existence. One cannot help but be in awe when he contemplates the mysteries of the Eternity, of life, of the marvelous structures of reality. It is enough if one tries merely to comprehend a little of this mystery each day. Also, I am enough of an Artist to draw freely upon my imagination. Imagination is more important than knowledge. Knowledge is limited. Imagination encircles the world.

Logic will get you from A to Z; imagination will get you every where! (in to Space and Time)

Vivi : "What is infinite?"

Einstein : "Tow things are infinite : The Universe and the Human stupididty; and I am not sure about the Universe."

Sabu : "Okay…Sir…What is life/."

Einstein : "Life is like bi-cycle. To keep your balance, you must keep moving."

Vivi : "Beautiful comparison …sir."

Sir…we have in mind to do a Big thing…We do not know whether we will succeed or not…What do you say for that…"

Einstein : "Simple. Anyone who had never made a mistake has ever tried anything new…"

Sabu : "Yes…sir. We have a plan to do a new thing.."

Einstein : "Go head. All the best."

Vivi : "Thank you, gentleman."

Sabu : "Sir…when did you present the famous equation $E=mc2$ and Theory of Relativity and other papers on Photo Electric effect?"

Einstein : "Annus Mirabalis…Wonderful year 1905!"

Vivi : "So 16 years has elapsed?"

Einstein : "Yes. Time runs."

Sabu : "Sir…A good news to you. You will be receiving the Noble Prize for Physics tomorrow…"

Vivi : "Yes…sir. Our advance Congratulations!"

Einstein : " What ? What???? ???

19. 2 Indians bag Noble Prizes for 2116!!

Nava Bharath Times reported as follows :

Two Nava Bharath Men (Indians) bag the Noble Prizes for the year 2116 A.D.!

Professor Rishi and Research Scholar Siddha of Nava Bharath have bagged the Noble Prize for Medicine (Genetic Engineering) and Chemistry respectively.

The details are as follows :

Research Scholar Siddha.

He is research scholar in CHEN University. (Old Madras University). He was awarded the Noble Prize for Chemistry for the year 2116. He is a Tamilian.

He was awarded the coveted prize for his invention of a new element. He named the element as SOORIYUM. It has chemical code SU3. Basically the new element Sooriyum is found in the inner space or core of the earth. It is present in a very, very high temperatures only. And this element is found abundantly in the star SUN too. In Tamil Sooriyum means 'SUN'. Since the Sun has Sooriyum apart from Hydrogen and Helium the element has been named as SOORIYUM!

It is a new kind of element. It is neither solid nor liquid nor gaseous. It is a combination of all the three forms of matter. That is why it is coded SU3. Triple in one! The beauty of this element is that it has a melting point of 7,00,0000C.

Wow! Wow!!

What does it mean?

The element can easily with stand the heat and the UV radiation of the Sun! That is the heat emitted by the Sun will have NO impact on the element!

Aha! Aha!! What an invention?

Hats off to Siddha!

PROFESSOR RISHI

He is native of KOL. (Old Kolkata). He is a professor in Genetics. He was awarded the coveted Noble Prize for the year 2116! Prof. Rishi has found out a new type of Surgery…that is Genetic surgery or Genetic Transfusion which will make the Humans longevity to deaths.

Aha! Aha!!

Yes…after the Genetic Transfusion a man live for NOT less than 200 years !

A Death to Death!!

Fabulous! Marvelous!!

Theory : Genes are the body's chemical instructions for your entire life-for growing up, surviving, having children and perhaps for dying. The Genes are sections of the nucleus acid called DNA (Deoxyribonucleic Acid)

It is not that the Gene are coded and it is they who give orders to cells (Organs) regularly. Prof.Rishi has identified a MAIN DNA which is responsible for living, aging and dying. And he has invented the new Anti Main Gene which will INSTRUCT and Command to the cells for not-aging and not-dying. His theory is proved clinically.

A man after Genetic Transfusion will live up to 200 years!

Aha! What an invention?

Salutations to Prof.Rishi.

Finally these 2 inventions in Chemistry and Genetics in the year 2116 is considered to be the Greatest inventions of the 22nd century. It is a Total Revolution. Humans have conquered the worst 'Death'!!

Rishi and Siddha will be remembered in our Galaxy, the Milky Way for millions of years to come.

Salutations to the both great Scientists!

Hearty Congrats!!

Nava Bharath is really Nava Bharath!!

A very NEW Bharath!!!

———— ◆ ————

20. ISRO!

Name   : Indian Space Research Organization

Abbreviation : I.S.R.O.

Acronym   : ISRO

Owner   : Nava Bharath. (India)

Motto   : Space Technology for the betterment

                of Humankind.

Accomplished : * 36 satellites

        * Chandrayan 1, 2, 3, 4, and 5
        * Chandrayan 5 landed human on Moon.
        * First attempt itself succeeded.
        * Mangalyan 1, 2, 3, 4, and 5
        * Mangalyan 5 landed Humans on Mars
        * First in the UNIVERSE!

Nest Project : GAV = Great Aadthiya Vaasam!

                A great voyage to SUN!!

Astronauts   : 2. One man and one woman

Progress   : Rigorous. Fast R & D. Great Going.

Action   : 2 Astronauts of Nava Bharath will

                float with a Tri-Colored

National Flag in the SUN.

Importance : First of its kind in the MILKY WAY!

In one Phrase : An ABSOLUTE REVOLUTION!

Fixed launch Time : **2216 A.D**.

———◆———

21. SAVI TRIP

E mail to : Mr. Viji Special officer, ISRO (7 O' 7)

Sub   : Urgent help

Respected Sir…

Our salutations to you. You as the special officer of 'Kala

Yantra' 7 O' 7 has given us a golden opportunity to Trave Time. We were excited and enjoyed our travel to different times to the core. We have recorded everything for the use in future. We know that 7 O' 7 is the first of its kind in the Planet.

We are really proud to have used that. We heartedly thank you for that. Coming to the point…

WE NEED URGENT HELP FROM YOU.

The machine 7 O' 7 will expire in 3 days time. We want to do something different and adventurous. Yes. We have planned a SAVI TRIP. Savi in Tamil means 'KEY'.

Yes. It is a key trip!

SAVI = SAbu + VIvi = SAVI Trip!

Sir…

By this time we think you would have come to know our thought and plan. Please treat this as HIGHLY CONFIDENTIAL till we return. Kindly oblige.

We know that there is No gain without No pain.

We know what we are going to do…

We are confident! We need am Urgent help from you. We have landed 7 O' 7 in the CHEN outlet of ISRO.

WE WANT…

No 1. To insulate the entire 7 O' 7 with 3 coats of colorless Sooriyum3 element!

No.2. We need a Tri-Color National Flag with same colorless coat of Sooriyum. SU3. And

No.3. We need 2 space suits insulated with the same element 3 times.

We prefer 3 time insulation for the safety reasons.

We hope our SAVI TRIP or KEY TRIP is clear to you. You are a genius and we hope you would have completely come to know about our Trip!

Yes.

The SAVI TRIP is to SUN!

You are 100% right!!

Lastly we need 2 Life boxes of Oxygen attached to our Space suits.

The SAVI Equation is as follows :

$$2\ CO_2 + 2H_2O \text{------------------} > C_2H_4 + 2(O_2)$$

One is Carbo-quadhyride and the other Oxygen. One molecule of Oxygen is again used for RE-CYCLING

$$C_2H_4 + O_2 \text{---------} \rightarrow = 2(H_2O) + C_2$$

So…Carbon is burnt. We have water and oxygen again and again.

Yes…Oxygen for our inhalation and Carbon-di-oxide is our exhalation. Water in vapor state is re-cycled.

Water in vapor state is used for re-cycled. We will get oxygen continuously.

For safety reasons let Oxygen go through 2 tubes…one through the nose and the other through the mouth.

That's all sir.

We want everything in a couple of days. We are browsing INTERNET and OUTERNET. Also we want to meditate and do yoga to prepare for the Key Trip.

So…day after tomorrow we will take off in 7 O' 7 (Insulated) to SUN!

Dear Sir….

Please provide us with what we need. We hope we will do the best. We have bagged Junior Scientist Award from ISRO. You must know that. We hope you will encourage us with your help and advice if any…

WE ARE IN TO THE FIRST OF ITS KIND IN THE HUMAN HISTORY…

Best Wishes,

Sabu-Vivi (SAVI), 2116.

22. A Great Leap Forward!!! & An Absolute Revolution???

7 0'7

"Vivi…Are You ready?"

"Yes…Sabu."

"See…if we travel to the speed of light…i.e. 1, 80,000kms/sec it will take 8 minutes and 26 seconds to reach the SUN."

"Ya..Sabu…switch on all the cameras…and also angular video graphs now itself…we must record everything right from now… Okay?"

"OK"

"Pray Almighty"

"Done"

"Start…Enter speed of light."

"Done"

O o o o o o o o o o o o o o o o o o o o
MMMMMmmmmmmmmmmmmmmmmmmmmmmmm!!!

O o o o o o o o o o o o o o o o o o o o
MMMMMMMMmmmmmmmmmmmmmmmmmmmmmmmm!!!

"Can you hear me?"

"Can you hear the unique sound?"

"Ya….OOOOOOOOOMMMMMMMMMMMMMMM"

"Ya…yes it is"

"See …we can stay in Sun's surface only for 3 minutes…that is 180 seconds. We should put 7 O' 7 in Sun's Revolutionary speed… Then 7 O' 7 will be 'stationery' for us. We should float or walk only for 160 seconds…"

"Ya…Within next 20 seconds…we must return to 7 O' 7!"

'Get Ready"

"Yes"

OOOOOOOOOOOOMMMMMMMMMMMMMMMMMM

OOOOOOOOOOOOOOOOOOOMMMMMMMMM MMMMM

7

6

5

4

3

2

1

O (Sun picture) SABU & VIVI FLOAT!

The Oxygen Box works nicely. They NEVER feel any HEAT. Both of then hold the National Flag in one hand and raises the fist of the other arm…showing victory.

It is Flame and Fire Everywhere!

Only 30 seconds left to return to 7 O' 7….

What a beauty? What a beauty?

'AADHITHYA VAHAGANAM' THE SPACE SHIP OF ISRO IS TOO ON THE SURFACE OF THE SUN. THE ORBITOR IS DE-CONNECTED TO THE MAIN VECHILE. THERE COMES 2 ASRTONAUTS TO WALK ON SUN!!!

One man.

One woman.

Man aged 108 years young.

Woman aged 113 years young.

YES…It is…

Sabu & Vivi ….

Oooooooh!

Oooooooh!!

VAV!!!

Sabu (108) and Vivi (!!) look at the IMPOSSIBLE… They take snaps at once. They are seeing 2 kids entering 7 O' 7.

Sabu(108) : "Hey…it is you and I"

Vivi(113) : "Humma…it is unimaginable…that is you and me…"

Sabu (108) : "We were 8 and 13 years 'OLD' then…"

Vivi (113) : "Ya…Sabu ….I do not know whether I am dreaming …?"

Sabu (108) : " No…Vivi…it is Real."

Vivi (113) : "Yes…I realize" and she shouts loud "HOWZAAT!"

Sabu (108) : "Vivi..it is Shock to me…'They'…no…no…'WE' have moved a GREAT LEAR FORWARD by 100 years in 7 O' 7! Ya! It is a Forward Travel of Time."

Vivi(113) : " You was 8 'then' and I was 13 'then'…or 'NOW'?"

Sabu (108) : "Ya…you were 13 'then'…or 'now'?"

Vivi : "Ooo! Ooo!! HOWZATTTT!"

Sabu : "Two parallel Lines meet at Infinity. Isn't it?"

Vivi : "Ya…that theory can be REALIZED 'NOW' ONLY…"

Sabu : "See…7 O' 7 is going back….and 'they' no…'we' are returning…"

Vivi : " WE have got 18 more minutes to stay here…let us do our job."

Sabu : "It is totally UNBELEIVABLE!"

Vivi : "TIME IS JUST SIMPLY GREAT AND GREAT!!!"

Sabu : "Aadhithya Vaasam" of ISRO proved to be very successful…

The mission of 2216 is Successful!"

Vivi : "AN ABSOLUTE REVOLUTION!"

Sabu : "Two parallel lines meet at infinity…It is PROVED."

00. 2116 !

7 O' 7

3

2

1

EEEEEEEEEZZZZZZZZZZZZZZ!!! !!! !

7 O' 7 landed back.

In the terrace of Shastha Apartments.

Sabu & Vivi come out shouting…..

"Mum and Dad…we have done that…"

"We are back from the Great SUN!"

It is 2116 A.D.!

Mind that it is 2116 A.D. only!!

Sabu is 8.

Vivi is 13.

7 O' 7 expires.

Good bye.

All that ends WELL.

Knowledge is Great

But Imagination is still Greater!